THE STAR FLEET

TEN CENTS
Stack no. 1 – Harbour Switcher
Captain Star's first tug.
Harbour-wise and very
experienced.

BIG MAC
Stack no. 2 – Harbour Tug
One of the biggest Star Tugs.
Strong and river-wise.

O.J.
Stack no. 3 – Paddle-wheel Harbour Tug
Oldest, wisest of the Star Tugs.
Versatile but slow-moving.

TOP HAT

Stack no. 4 – Railway Tug
Only Star Tug with a
raised wheelhouse.
Tries to avoid any
dirty work.

WARRIOR

Stack no. 5 – Harbour Tug
Very strong, but
sometimes clumsy.
Will tackle any job.

HERCULES

Stack no. 6 – Ocean-going Tug
One of the leaders of the fleet.
Very proud and rather aloof.

SUNSHINE

Stack no. 7 – Harbour Switcher
Newest member of the Star Fleet.
Works mainly with Ten Cents.

William Heinemann Ltd
Michelin House
81 Fulham Road
London SW3 6RB
LONDON   MELBOURNE   AUCKLAND
Text copyright © 1989 William Heinemann Ltd
Photographs copyright © 1989 Clearwater Merchandising Ltd
TUGS is produced by TUGS Ltd for Clearwater Features
(1986) Ltd and TVS Television, copyright © TUGS 1988
ISBN (HB) 434 95013 0 (PB) 434 95009 2
Based on **Ghosts**, an episode of the television series TUGS
created by Robert D Cardona and David Mitton.
Ghosts was written and directed by David Mitton and
produced by Robert D Cardona.
Photographs by Terry Permane.
Artwork by Stephen Lings and William O'Keefe.
Script adapted by Penny Morris. Designed by Fiona Macmillan.
Printed in Great Britain by Cambus Litho, East Kilbride

Ghost Fleet

In the 1920s tugboats played a very important part in the harbour life of all international ports. Although small, they had very powerful engines and were responsible for moving all kinds of vessels around the harbour and docks, from huge liners and cargo ships to barges and dredgers.
In Bigg City port, there were two tugboat companies operating – the Star Fleet, owned by Captain Star, and the Z Stacks, owned by Captain Zero. The two fleets were constantly competing for business, the Star Tugs by honest means. However the Z Stacks were not always so honourable...

Heinemann · London

Bigg City port was in the grip of winter. It had come earlier than expected and with it came the fog.

The Star Tugs hated the fog – in those days they had no radio or radar. They had to rely on eyes and ears, and the fog could sometimes play tricks on those.

Long periods of fog had a way of conjuring up old sea stories and superstitions among the boats of the harbour. Many of the tugs felt nervous in the daytime fog. When darkness fell, they became even more anxious and a little bit jumpy.

On this particular evening, Big Mac was on his way back to the Star Pier. He'd been working all day with Scuttle Butt Pete, who had been telling him old sea stories, about the strange things that could happen when fog was around.

As Big Mac passed a spooky old warehouse, he heard a whispering sound. The buildings creaked and groaned as though they were alive.

The whispering sound grew louder. Big Mac peered through the fog but couldn't see anything.

"This is too creepy for me," he muttered. "I'm getting home fast, fog or no fog." He set off through the fog but suddenly, there in front of him, appeared four ghostly white tugs.

"Aaah!" gulped Big Mac. "It's the ghost fleet that Scuttle Butt Pete was talking about."

It was all too much for Big Mac. He turned and charged off through the fog hoping the ghost fleet was not following him, and eventually reached the safety of the Star Pier.

All the Star Tugs except Hercules were in their berths as Big Mac came steaming in.

"Slow down, Big Mac," said Top Hat. "You know better than to travel that fast in fog."

O.J. looked closely at Big Mac. "You all right, Big Mac?" he asked. "You look as though you've seen a ghost!"

"Well, er, actually, I have," said Big Mac in a shaky voice.

"You've seen what?" asked Warrior.

"Ghosts," replied Big Mac.

"Well, well," laughed Top Hat. "I never thought a harbour tug would believe in ghosts!"

The other tugs joined in the laughter, as Big Mac looked embarrassed.

Early the next morning, Captain Star gave his fleet their orders for the day. The fog was still very thick, and as the tugs prepared to go to work, they teased Big Mac about his 'ghost'.

"I shouldn't have told you," scowled Big Mac.

"You take no notice," said O.J. "The fog plays funny tricks on all of us. Don't you worry about it, Big Mac. Just mind you keep your wits about you."

Big Mac moved off muttering to himself. "I suppose I could've been seeing things. But they seemed jolly real at the time, I can tell you."

The tugs set to work.

That evening, Warrior was making his way back to the Star Pier across the bay. The fog was still thick so he sounded his foghorn frequently. Some shrimpers were following him, using him to guide them in to the port.

"Hey, Warrior," called one of the shrimpers. "Are you sure you know the way?"

"Of course," grinned Warrior. "A bit of fog is nothing to worry about. I've got a natural sense of direction. Just stick close to me and . . . oops!" Warrior had to swerve violently to avoid a mudbank.

The shrimpers behind him were not so lucky. They ran straight into the mudbank and stuck there.

Warrior steamed happily along, then suddenly jerked to a halt. There in front of him were four white tugs.

"What the . . . ?" Warrior watched in horror as the tugs moved across in front of him.

"Who are they? I don't believe it," he thought. "It's just as Big Mac said. It's the ghost fleet!"

He hurried back to the Star Pier to tell the others.

Further out in the bay Izzy Gomez, the tramp steamer, had been waiting all day for a cheap tow into the harbour. As night fell, he decided to try and sneak into the harbour for free, under cover of the fog.

Just as he started to lift his anchor, Zorran, the leader of the Z Stacks, appeared.

"You never learn, do you Izzy," sneered Zorran. "Breaking the law as usual. Well, if you run aground, you'll be my salvage."

"No salvage," replied Izzy. "I'll give you fifty to tow me in."

"Get lost," said Zorran. "You're worth more to me as scrap!" and he moved off into the fog.

Izzy pulled up his anchor the rest of the way and set off for the harbour.

But as Zorran moved across the bay he saw something up ahead.

"Ahoy!" he called. "Do you need a tow into port?"

There was no reply.

Zorran watched in horror as four white tugs appeared through the fog and sailed past him.

"It's the ghosts! Big Mac's ghosts," cried Zorran, "they've come to get me!" and he turned round and steamed back the way he had come as fast as he could.

Back in the bay, Izzy was just beginning to move.

"It's very foggy," he muttered to himself, "so if I can't see anybody, then nobody can see me. I'll get into port for free for once. Ha! That's good!"

He caught sight of something coming towards him.

"Hey, watch where you're going," he yelled and sounded his horn.

There was no reply, as four white tugs slid silently by.

"Help!" cried Izzy. "It's ghosts! Don't take me! I've got a tow already! Please don't take me!"

As the ghost tugs disappeared into the mists, Izzy turned towards the harbour again and bumped into Zorran, who was going round in circles in the fog.

"Zorran!" cried Izzy, with relief. "Give me a tow. I'll pay whatever you want. Just get me into port!"

"No problem, Izzy my old friend," said Zorran. "I'll tow you in for nothing. I need some company!"

That night was a terrible night for the Star Tugs. Even level-headed old O.J. thought he saw the ghosts. As he was returning from escorting two tramp steamers out to sea, he decided to cut through the inlet where the old cranes were kept.

The fog gave everything a creepy look and the sounds of rattling chains and grinding metal made O.J. uneasy.

"It's just the fog playing tricks on me," O.J. muttered to himself as he hurried along. "Drat this fog. I can't see a thing. Oooops! What's that?" He had nearly run into Scuttle Butt Pete.

"You stupid tug," cried Scuttle Butt. "Oh, it's you, O.J. You nearly scared the daylights out of me!"

"Thought I was a ghost tug, did you?" said O.J. "You're beginning to believe those tales you tell!"

"Don't joke about such things," warned Scuttle Butt Pete. "You take care."

As O.J. continued on his way, he heard a sound behind him. He glanced back and, to his horror, saw the ghostly shapes of four white tugs moving through the fog.

"Oh no! Now I'm seeing things. No, they're really there! It's the ghost tugs!" and he set off at top speed back to the Star Pier.

In the harbour, quite near to the Star Pier, Top Hat was on his way home. He had been out in the fog all day and was feeling quite anxious.

"That's funny," he thought. "I don't recognise a thing. Can't even hear any foghorns." He steamed along keeping close to the shoreline, hoping to see a familiar landmark.

Suddenly, he saw two bright pinpoints of light ahead of him.

"What's that? I never thought I'd get as jittery as the others, but I am. Where am I?"

He looked all around. "If I steer between those trampers I should be in open water," but as he glanced through the gap, he couldn't believe his eyes . . .

"Oh no! It's the ghost fleet! It's true!"

The white tugs moved away through the fog.

"That's enough for me," trembled Top Hat. "I'm staying here until daylight. It's too dangerous out there. I'll dock here and find my way back in the morning."

He settled down for an uneasy night's sleep.

Out in the estuary, Ten Cents and Sunshine were towing an oil barge towards Lillie Lightship.

"If we don't get to her soon, her light may go out," said Sunshine, anxiously.

"We'll make it," said Ten Cents.

There was a loud cracking sound ahead of them.

"What's that?" cried Sunshine.

The noise grew louder.

"I don't like it, Ten Cents. What's happening?"

"Sounds like ice cracking, but it can't be at this time of year, can it?"

"How should I know. I've never seen anything like this before," replied Ten Cents nervously.

"Our number's up. They've come to get us."

The sea ahead of them began to bubble and suddenly, up out of the water appeared an old galleon.

"Look at that!" gasped Ten Cents.

"It's a ghostly galleon," wavered Sunshine, and together the two terrified tugs turned and charged away through the fog.

The following morning the sun came up and blazed through the thinning fog.

Top Hat was still asleep where he'd tied up, when Grampus the midget submarine, surfaced beside him and spouted water on his face.

"No, don't hurt me, go away ghosts," cried Top Hat as he woke up with a start. "Oh, it's you Grampus."

"What are you doing here, Top Hat?" asked Grampus. "And what's this about ghosts?"

"Did I say ghosts?" laughed Top Hat. "I must have been dreaming. I lost my bearings in the fog and couldn't get home, so I moored here for the night."

Grampus laughed. "Here? But you're only a few minutes from home. Look!"

Top Hat look around. The Star Pier was just across the way. So he'd nearly been home after all!

At the Star Pier, all the other tugs were in their berths except Hercules. Top Hat steamed up.

"Listen everyone. I've seen the ghost tugs. Really!"

"We've all seen them, Top Hat," said O.J. "Ten Cents and Sunshine saw a galleon, too."

"But these were real ghosts," insisted Top Hat. "Phantoms of the seas!"

There was a loud hoot and Hercules steamed up.

"Ghosts?" smiled Hercules. "What's this about ghosts?"

"Ghostly white tugs . . . " said Big Mac.

"And a galleon," added Ten Cents.

Hercules laughed. "You're all seeing things. If I'd been here I'd have explained things. Those tugs you saw are the white fleet, down here from northern waters. They're on the trail of an iceberg which has floated down here and is a danger to ships. There was an old galleon frozen in the iceberg. I suppose when the ice finally melted the old boat bobbed up to the surface."

Behind Hercules, Burke and Blair steamed past, towing the old galleon.

"There's your ghostly galleon, Ten Cents," laughed Hercules.

The Star Tugs watched as Burke and Blair towed away the old galleon. A moment later the white fleet steamed past on their way back up north, their job done.

The Star Fleet laughed about it, relieved to hear the simple explanation, but they never forgot the time the fog made them see ghosts!

THE Z STACKS

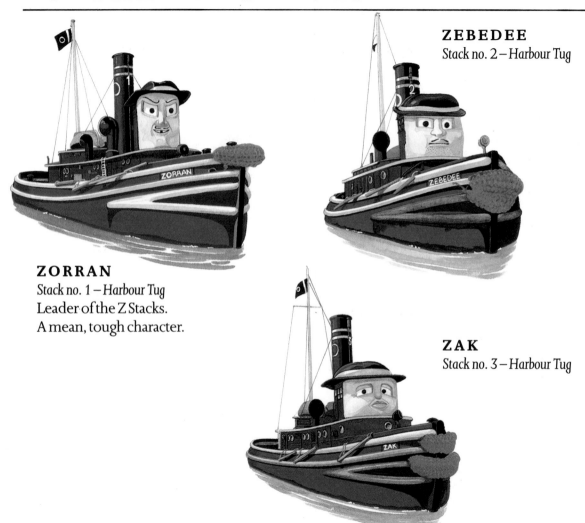

ZEBEDEE
Stack no. 2 – Harbour Tug

ZORRAN
Stack no. 1 – Harbour Tug
Leader of the Z Stacks.
A mean, tough character.

ZAK
Stack no. 3 – Harbour Tug

ZUG
Stack no. 4 – Harbour Switcher

LILLIE
LIGHTSHIP

ZIP
Stack no. 5 – Harbour Switcher

GRAMPUS
A midget submarine

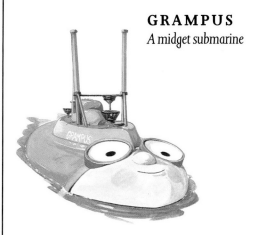